I like to spin!

The kids pick on Fran.

Frogs can't spin.

I can spin. Look!
And I can flip, too!

Frogs can't flip.

I like to flip.

Go, Fran!

Fran slips.

Oh, no!
Oh, my!

See, you can't spin.
You can't flip.

Sniff, sniff.
I can't flip.

Yes, you can.

Fran spins.
She flips.
She did it!

See!
Frogs *can* spin
and flip.

We like the flip, Fran!

I did it!
Yes, Fran,
you did it!

Target Letter-Sound Correspondence

Consonant /f/ sound spelled ***f***

Previously Introduced Letter-Sound Correspondences:

Consonant /s/ sound spelled ***s***
Consonant /m/ sound spelled ***m***
Short /ă/ sound spelled ***a***
Consonant /k/ sound spelled ***c***
Consonant /n/ sound spelled ***n***
Consonant /k/ sound spelled ***k, ck***
Consonant /z/ sound spelled ***s***
Consonant /t/ sound spelled ***t***
Consonant /p/ sound spelled ***p***
Short /ŏ/ sound spelled ***o***
Consonant /g/ sound spelled ***g***
Consonant /d/ sound spelled ***d***
Short /ĭ/ sound spelled ***i***
Consonant /r/ sound spelled ***r***
Consonant /l/ sound spelled ***l***
Consonant /h/ sound spelled ***h***

High-Frequency Puzzle Words

go	she
like	the
likes	to
look	**too**
my	we
no	yes
oh	you
see	

Bold indicates new high-frequency word.